First published in Great Britain 2018 by Child's Play (International) Ltd
Ashworth Road, Bridgemead, Swindon SN5 7YD, UK

Dual language edition first published in 2019 by Mantra Lingua
Global House, 303 Ballards Lane, London N12 8NP
www.mantralingua.com

This dual language edition published 2021

ISBN 978-1-78784-704-0
Printed in UK

A catalogue record of this book
is available from the British Library

MANTRA
LINGUA

El Jardín de Errol

Errol's GARDEN

GILLIAN HIBBS

Spanish translation by Marta Belén Sáez Cabero

Se me da muy bien cultivar cosas.

I'm really good at growing things.

¡Se me da tan
bien que empezamos
a quedarnos sin
espacio en casa!

I'm so good at it
that we started
running out of
room at home!

Lo que yo quería era un jardín de verdad.

What I really wanted was a real garden.

Me pasaba el día pensando en mi jardín.

I dreamed about my garden a lot.

Pero un día,
noté algo que nunca
había visto antes.

Then one day,
I noticed something
I'd never seen
before.

Siempre había creído que
vivíamos en el último piso,
pero había otro botón…

I always thought that
we lived on the top floor,
but there was another button…

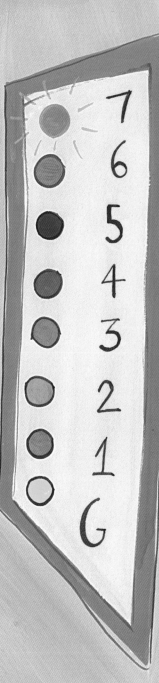

¡… y había una azotea!

¡Me parecía increíble
que no la hubiera
visto antes!

...and there was a roof!

I couldn't believe
I hadn't seen it before!

Éste era el sitio
perfecto para el jardín.

This was the perfect
spot for the garden.

Se lo dije a Papá y a Tía enseguida.

I told Dad and Tia right away.

Aprendimos muchísimo acerca
de jardines en azoteas.

We learned as much as we could
about roof gardens.

Pero necesitábamos ayuda.
¡Por suerte, todo el mundo estaba tan entusiasmado como yo!

But we needed help.
Luckily, everyone else was just as excited as me!

Hicimos un plano.

We made a plan.

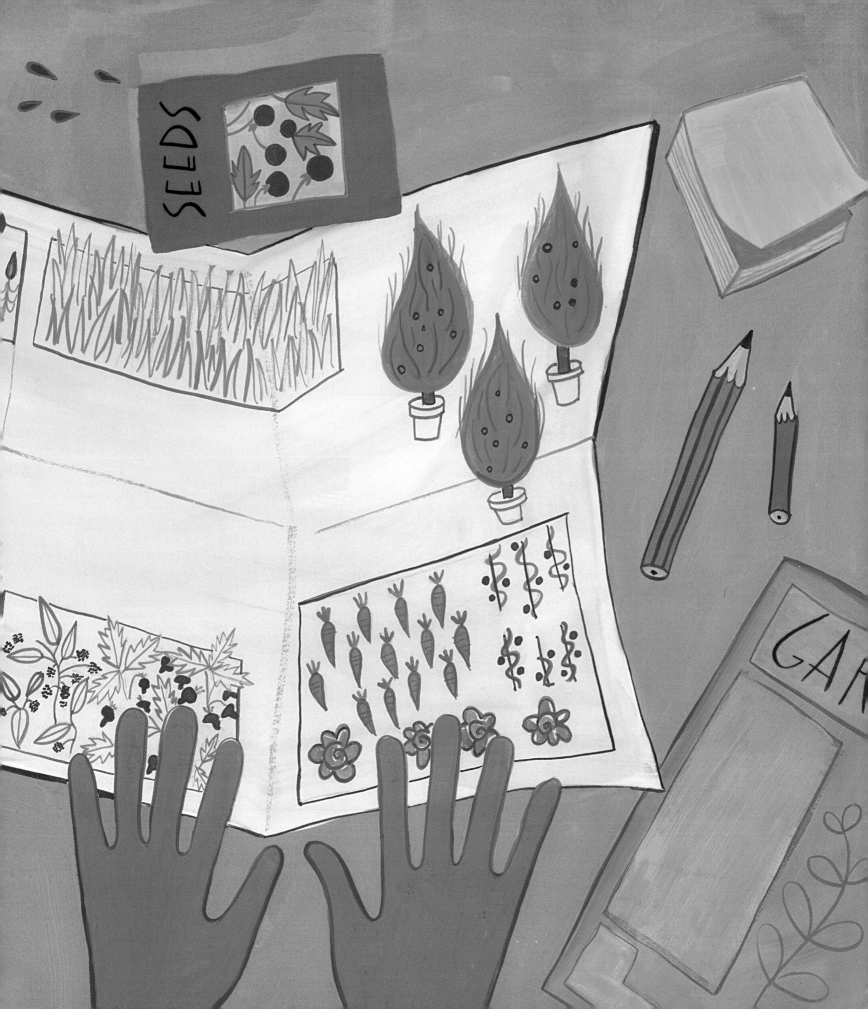

Todo el mundo tenía ideas diferentes,
lo cual está muy bien…

Everyone had different things to bring...
which was good...

...porque había muchísimo que hacer.

...because there were lots of different things to do.

¡Y todavía lo hay!

Me encanta recolectar la fruta y las verduras.

And there still are!

I love picking all the fruit and vegetables.

¡Me encantan las zanahorias!　　　I really love carrots!

Los jardines son muy
entretenidos porque siempre
están cambiando.

Gardens are fun because
they are always changing.

Así que, ¿qué cultivaremos el año que viene?

So, what will we grow next year?

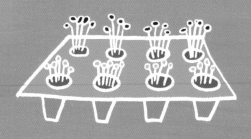